# The Cooking Contest

by Kathy Furgang

illustrated by Stan Tusan

## Table of Contents

# The Contest

It was a lazy summer afternoon. Lisa was visiting her friend James. They had already played a video game, kicked around a soccer ball, and searched for lizards in the backyard. Now they were bored.

"I'm bored," said Lisa.

"Me too," said James. "I wish there was something fun to do."

"Here's something you might be interested in," said James's mom. She was reading a stack of mail. "The neighborhood block party is next week. There will be a cooking contest! It says here that they want to put the most creative recipes into a neighborhood cookbook."

"Hey, that's it!" said Lisa. "We can make up a recipe! That would be fun."

"I want to help!" yelled James's little sister, Tina, bouncing up and down.

"No way, Tina. You don't know how to cook. You're just a baby," said James.

"Am not!" said Tina.

"Are too!" said James.

"Quit fighting, kids," said James's mom. "Why don't you all enter the contest together?"

James and Lisa looked at each other. "I think there's going to be trouble," said James.

# Fun in the Kitchen

"If we're going to win this contest, we need to be different," said Lisa. "I want the judges to notice us."

"How?" asked James.

"We need to create something special and delicious that kids will love to eat," Lisa replied.

James thought a moment. "Like what?" he asked.

"Snacks!" suggested Tina.

James was about to tell Tina to be quiet, when Lisa said, "That's not a bad idea, Tina. Everybody loves snacks—especially kids. We're kids, so we should be experts on what kids like to eat!"

Tina beamed.

"You're going to listen to my sister?" asked James.

"Sure," Lisa replied. "Think about it, James. Everybody else is going to cook something boring, like vegetable soup. But we want our recipe to be exciting!"

"Yeah!" screamed Tina. "Exciting!"

Lisa and James searched through the kitchen cabinets. "Oh! I have an excellent idea," said James excitedly.

"Me too," said Lisa, tying on an apron. Tina grabbed some things from the bottom cabinets and ran into the backyard. They each got to work, making up their own recipes. They created and measured and mixed.

# The Snacks

A few minutes later, James and Lisa were ready to show each other their delicious snack creations. James presented his bowl to Lisa.

"What is that?" Lisa asked James.

"I call it the Mega-Monster Mix. It's Animal Oaties cereal, fishy crackers, butter, Sugar Poppers, and of course, ketchup," James replied proudly.

"Is it supposed to taste like this?" asked Lisa.

"I'm not really sure," said James, making a face.

"Well, here's my new snack creation," said Lisa. "It's an ice cream sandwich mashed up with popcorn, mustard, applesauce, lettuce, and marshmallows."

James peered into the bowl. He picked it up and gave it a sniff. "*Yuck*! Lisa, no kid I know is going to eat this."

Tina ran into the kitchen and put a shovel and pail on the table. The pail was filled with a mixture of dirt, leaves, rocks, lemonade mix, and crunchy peanut butter.

"*Ugh*! Disgusting! Tina, you can't eat that. It's not even food!" said James.

"It's mine and you can't have it," Tina sniffed. She reached up to the counter for an ice cream cone. She scooped the mixture into the cone with the shovel.

"Maybe the crunchy peanut butter and the ice cream cone aren't such bad ideas," said Lisa.

"Are you kidding?" said James. "You're listening to my sister again?"

"Let's take some things that each of us used and make a whole new snack," said Lisa. "We can even call it Mega-Monster Mix. We can use a pail and shovel to serve it on a cone."

Animal
Oaties
cereal

fishy
crackers

popcorn

peanut
butter

marshmallows

16

# Making the Recipe

The children tried the recipe with a little of this and a lot of that. Finally, they had a mixture that they all agreed tasted delicious. It was time to write down the recipe for the contest.

"I can't figure this out," said James. "How do we write this recipe? We used Animal Oaties cereal, fishy crackers, popcorn, peanut butter, and marshmallows. We just mashed the Mega-Monster Mix together in a pail and shoveled it into an ice cream cone."

"We have to explain how much of each food to use in one whole batch of Mega-Monster Mix," said Lisa. "We can write it as fractions."

Lisa took out paper and a pencil. "Let's draw all the cups of food we used. That might help us see how to write it," she said.

"There are five different foods that go into the Mega-Monster Mix. We used the same amount of each food. Each food is one-fifth of the whole mix," said Lisa. "So the recipe is to use one-fifth Animal Oaties cereal, one-fifth fishy crackers, one-fifth popcorn, one-fifth marshmallows, and one-fifth crunchy peanut butter. That's one whole Mega-Monster Mix!"

"And it doesn't even matter what size cup you use," added James. "There will always be one-fifth of each food, so it will always taste the same."

# Time for the Judges

Lisa, James, and Tina all had a great time at the block party. They played games and won prizes. Their favorite prize of the day was for the Mega-Monster Mix. They each won a ribbon that said, "First Prize! Most Interesting Food."

"I can't wait to see your recipe in the cookbook!" said the judge.